THERE'S A
HAMSTER
IN MY
LUNCHBOX

THERE'S A HAMSTER IN MY LUNCHBOX

by SUSAN CLYMER ■ Illustrated by PAUL CASALE

A
LITTLE APPLE
PAPERBACK

SCHOLASTIC INC.
New York Toronto London Auckland Sydney

No part of this publication may be reproduced in whole or in part, or stored in a retrieval system, or transmitted in any form or by any means, electronic, mechanical, photocopying, recording, or otherwise, without written permission of the publisher. For information regarding permission, write to Scholastic Inc., 555 Broadway, New York, NY 10012.

ISBN 0-590-48120-7

22 21 20 19 18 17   23/0

Printed in the U.S.A.   40

First Scholastic printing, September 1994

To Richard Wayne Clymer,
a wonderful older brother

Contents

1	The Mystery Begins	1
2	Little Sister!	11
3	Tickled by a Hamster	17
4	A Two-Color Family	29
5	The Squeakmobile	33
6	The Great Escape	47
7	"No Touch Hamster"	57
8	Flashlight in the Night	63
9	Promises	69
10	The Carnival	79
11	Squeaks's Greatest Trick	91
12	The Unexpected Discovery	97
13	Show and Tell	109
14	Christmas!	117

1
The Mystery Begins

Elizabeth straightened her pointed black hat and shook her long cape. She *loved* Halloween. "Out of my way!" she warned. "I'm not very good at steering this broom!" Elizabeth swooped in front of the dragon standing at the school doors. She had been appointed jump rope monitor this week, so she had to be first in line.

Janna roared back at Elizabeth. Janna wore a green-and-purple dragon costume, her best disguise since she'd been a bumblebee in kindergarten. She had been pretending to capture people all recess.

Micah stood next to Elizabeth, holding a muddy soccer ball as far away as possible from his clean white doctor's coat. He had Popsicle sticks arranged in his pocket, and he wore a stethoscope around his neck.

Elizabeth and Micah led the way into Martin Luther King, Jr. Elementary. Just inside their classroom door, Elizabeth slid to a stop. She pointed at a strange box with wire sides sitting on the teacher's desk. Elizabeth would always remember later that she had been the first to see the cage.

"Look at that rat!" Micah exclaimed. "I mean mouse. I mean hamster! Oh, who would *dress up* a rodent?"

The fluffy orange animal wore a black cape and was racing around and around on a wheel inside the cage. Its tiny cape sailed out behind in the air.

The students and Mr. Jenkins pushed forward to surround the cage. "Great jumping grasshoppers!" the teacher muttered, slapping his red-and-white-striped pants

My naMe is Squeaks
I'M a six-week-old Teddy Bear HaMster
I'M a girl

and tugging at the little beard from his Uncle Sam's costume. "What is that animal doing on my desk?" The class could always tell when Mr. Jenkins was excited, because he talked in funny sayings.

Elizabeth read aloud the small sign that had been taped on the cage. The sign had been printed in green ink.

My naMe is Squeaks
I'M a six-week-old Teddy Bear HaMster
I'M a girl

Someone had tied black-and-orange crepe paper to the corners of the cage. A tiny broom leaned up against a square boxlike house inside. The house had been made all of Legos and had a perfect door and a little window, so the hamster could crawl in and out.

"Squeaks is a witch, just like Lizzy," Janna said.

Elizabeth didn't like being called Lizzy, but she ignored her friend. Janna was just being a troublesome dragon today. Squeaks stopped running and looked right at Elizabeth. The hamster had long golden and white fur . . . like a miniature lion. Elizabeth had never seen a long-haired hamster before.

The teddy bear hamster climbed off the wheel and sat up on her back feet. Her golden nose twitched. She licked her front paws and washed her face. Her ears weren't pointed like most animals. They were rounded and very thin. They looked like itsy-bitsy baseball mitts. "Aw, you're beautiful," Elizabeth whispered.

Mr. Jenkins's giant stuffed rabbit was leaning halfway over the cage, as if she were saying hello to the new arrival.

"I bet Santa Claus brought this hamster." David lifted his alien hands in the air. He had tied an extra finger to each hand for his red Martian costume. "Poof!" David cried. "Santa Claus landed on the school roof and sent two of his elves in here with the cage."

Mr. Jenkins ruffled David's pipe cleaner antennae. "It isn't Christmas. It's Halloween."

"Jeffrey could have brought her," Micah suggested seriously. Jeffrey was a boy from Mr. Jenkins's last year's class who often came to visit.

Elizabeth knew their teacher loved to tease. Mr. Jenkins could have sneaked the hamster in the room himself. Why . . . last week, right before they had first started studying African animals, Mr. Jenkins had announced that he had seen a giraffe by the principal's office. He had pretended to be serious!

The hamster started racing on her squeaky wheel again. She had a water bottle in her cage and an overflowing bowl of seeds.

"Can we keep her?" David and Janna begged.

"Can we adopt her?" Elizabeth asked softly. She knew all about adoption. She had been born in Central America in a country called Honduras. Mom had adopted her when she was a baby. Her little sister had been adopted, too.

Mr. Jenkins squeezed Elizabeth's shoulder. "We have a mystery to solve first, before we make any decisions." The teacher unlatched the cage door. "In the meantime, we have to take good care of this animal. We'd better start by removing the cape. It could get caught on the side of the cage or the wheel."

Squeaks stopped running and stared up at the teacher. She had beady little black eyes.

Mr. Jenkins reached for her. Squeaks zipped off her wheel. Mr. Jenkins gripped the hamster around the belly. Squeaks wriggled free and hid in the corner of the cage. "Come here, you little wiggle wort!"

The children laughed.

Mr. Jenkins grabbed for the hamster again. The teacher's face reddened, and he hopped backward. "That hamster tried to nip me!"

"Ah, she's scared." Without thinking, Elizabeth reached into the cage. Anybody would be scared who had to go to a new home. Her little sister had sure been scared when she'd arrived on the plane from Honduras.

Elizabeth plucked the cape with two fingers. The hamster backed away and slipped her neck out of the cape. Elizabeth's fingers brushed the soft fur. "Here, Mr. Jenkins." She held out the cape.

Squeaks looked right at Elizabeth as if to say, "That feels better." Then she streaked into her miniature house.

"Thanks, Elizabeth." Mr. Jenkins firmly hooked the cage door closed. "Sit down now, class. It's time for our Halloween math."

The children headed noisily toward their seats. Elizabeth dropped the jump rope in the outdoor box by the coats. Micah held the muddy soccer ball cradled against his white coat. He must have forgotten about the dirt.

Mr. Jenkins walked inside the giant U

pattern of their desks, placing a little bag of M&M's on each desk. He caught David's wrist as a piece of candy headed for his mouth. "Remember what we discussed before recess, children. I don't want you to eat your M&M's. I want you to count them by color and make your graph. Next, we'll make a class M&M's graph. After that, we get to eat our Halloween treats."

Elizabeth's desk was closest to the hamster. She wished she could really stroke her. Elizabeth noticed something odd about the handwriting on the sign. All the M's were written as capitals.

My naMe is Squeaks
I'M a six-week-old Teddy Bear HaMster

The hamster clambered out the window of her Lego house and headed for her wheel. She sure loved to run. The wheel turned and squeaked. Elizabeth snapped her fingers. That must be why the animal had been named Squeaks! Elizabeth grinned as she arranged her M&M's by color on her desktop.

The hamster climbed up the corner of the wire cage nearest Elizabeth's desk. She nibbled on the wire. "How did you get to our classroom?" Elizabeth muttered. "You didn't just fly here. Even if you are a witch . . . like me."

At that very moment, Elizabeth decided that she wanted to be the one to solve this mystery. Someone had given away this hamster, and she wanted to know who . . . and why. Squeaks twitched her nose and long whiskers as if she were smelling the chocolate.

"You and me, Squeaks," Elizabeth whispered, popping a green M&M into her mouth when the teacher wasn't looking. Too bad hamsters couldn't talk.

2
Little Sister!

Late that night, Elizabeth climbed into her bed and snapped on her flashlight to count her Halloween candy. She couldn't even turn on a lamp in her own bedroom after *seven-thirty* since her little sister had started sharing her room last month.

Luckily, Hillary didn't stir. She lay with her head on her stuffed alligator at the foot of the bed and her feet on her pillow. For the first two years, Hillary had slept in a crib in their dining room that Mom had remade into a nursery. Now she slept *here*.

Mom even called it Elizabeth and Hillary's room.

Elizabeth lined up the candy on her bed. She counted six chocolate bars, seventeen lollipops, eight pieces of gum. She had more candy than she'd ever had before. She and Janna and Janna's dad had walked every street in the neighborhood tonight.

Elizabeth crunched a sour lemon drop. All evening, she had wished the new little teddy bear hamster could be with her, dressed in her own witch's costume. Squeaks would have looked so cute, sitting on her shoulder or on the brim of her hat. They could have been a Big Witch and a Little Witch, out trick-or-treating together. For years, Elizabeth had wanted a pet, but Mom didn't think she was old enough.

She now had twelve piles of candy on her bed, ninety-three pieces altogether. Elizabeth divided in her head. If she ate three pieces a day, her candy could last over thirty days, all the way until Thanksgiving!

Something touched her elbow in the

darkness. Elizabeth jumped and nearly yelped.

"Candy?" a little voice asked. "Me, candy?" Hillary stood at her elbow, pointing. She wore her gray elephant pajamas with feet.

Elizabeth had been so busy counting that she hadn't heard her sister getting out of bed. Now what could she do? Elizabeth sighed. If she told Hillary she couldn't have any candy, she would wail. Then Mom would come into the room. Elizabeth knew *she'd* get in trouble for still being awake and maybe for having the camping flashlight up here.

Besides, Hillary's dark brown eyes were so wide open. The candy must look wonderful to her. They didn't get many sweets around here, that was for sure. Elizabeth carefully picked out a soft candy bar so her sister wouldn't choke. She even unwrapped it. Then she sent Hillary back to bed.

Elizabeth stuffed her candy back in her bag. Before she turned off the flashlight, she shone the light on her sister. Hillary had chocolate all over her chin and even on her nose. Elizabeth tiptoed across the room and wiped off her sister's face with a tissue.

Hillary held out her chubby arms. "Kiss."

Elizabeth didn't want to give her a kiss, but then again she didn't want to argue. She kissed her sister's cheek and climbed back into bed. Hillary started humming to herself.

Elizabeth hugged her Halloween bag. She wished Hillary hadn't seen the candy. There were times that a big sister needed privacy, and counting Halloween candy was one of those times.

She lay in the darkness for a long while. Elizabeth couldn't stop thinking about the fun she and Janna had had tonight. Then she started wondering about Squeaks.

Finally, she turned on her flashlight under her covers. Elizabeth read a story from *Mrs. Piggle-Wiggle* for the third time and licked a cherry lollipop.

3
Tickled by a Hamster

Elizabeth dragged herself to school the next morning. When her mother had called her at 7 A.M., all she'd wanted to do was go back to sleep . . . until she'd remembered today's famous kickball game against the fourth-graders.

By the time Elizabeth got to her room, a group of students and the teacher had already gathered around the hamster cage. Janna had one hand over her mouth, trying not to giggle.

Elizabeth hurried closer. Mr. Jenkins's giant stuffed rabbit was leaning crookedly over the hamster cage. One of the rabbit's ears now hung partway through the wire top. Inside the little hamster house was a new soft bed of stuffing. Squeaks lay on her back on the bed with her tummy exposed and her paws tucked under her chin. The hamster looked *very* cozy. She must have climbed to the top of the cage and chewed up the rabbit's ear. Then she'd carried the stuffing bit by bit into her house.

Mr. Jenkins was tapping the eraser of his pencil on his desk. *Tap, tap, TAP!* Everybody knew he had won that rabbit for his daughter by throwing a hoop over the tallest bottle at the county fair. Now his daughter was grown up, in high school. "I'll mend you tonight, Stuffy," he muttered and moved his prized possession to the bookcase.

When the bell rang, Mr. Jenkins made an announcement. "Our mystery *nibbling* visitor has changed our plans. I've decided

we are going to create a class book about hamsters."

Elizabeth sat up straighter. She liked making books.

"The librarian has given us permission to use the library this morning for research." Mr. Jenkins tossed a piece of chalk into the air and caught it. "I want each of you to choose a subject and write one page. Next week, you'll present your page aloud."

The whole class spent half an hour picking topics, like hamster food and hamster families. Then Mr. Jenkins asked everyone to sit down in the reading circle. Cut-out characters from books that the children had read hung on strings from the ceiling.

Elizabeth blew on the cut-out of Mrs. Piggle-Wiggle she had made as the teacher explained that observing meant watching closely. "Observing is an excellent way to learn about animal behavior." Mr. Jenkins asked them to stretch out their legs with their feet touching, to make a giant star on the reading circle carpet. "This will be our hamster-viewing pen . . . hopefully escape-proof."

Most of the girls had on long pants, but the few who wore dresses had shorts under them. Elizabeth sat next to Janna on one side and Brian on the other. Mr. Jenkins set Squeaks down in the middle of the star. She looked awfully little.

The sleepy hamster stood still for a moment. She scratched her fat tummy with one back foot. She did look a bit like a teddy bear. Then she waddled toward Micah. The hamster poked her head right into the ankle opening of his slacks. "Hey!" Micah's voice shot up. "Those are *my* pants!"

Squeaks backed away, startled. The whole class screeched. The hamster flattened herself and scurried under Micah's ankle . . . right out of the "escape-proof" star. She raced toward the coats. Her fluffy back end hair waved behind her like a tutu.

"I'll catch her!" Tom dove gracefully for

the hamster. He was studying ballet. He scooped her up just before she got to the lunch boxes under the coat hooks.

Tom and the teacher put Squeaks back in the center of the star. This time Squeaks ran straight for Elizabeth and climbed up on her lap. "Hi!" Elizabeth cried, delighted. She stroked the furry back with one finger. Squeaks tried to run off one side of her lap, but Janna blocked her way. Then Squeaks zipped to the other side of her lap.

David slapped his red high-topped tennis shoes against the floor. "Maybe Squeaks likes Elizabeth because she's the closest kid to hamster size."

Elizabeth gritted her teeth. She didn't like it when people teased her about being small. Mom said that most people born in Honduras were just littler than most people in the United States, so she'd probably be short all her life. Then Elizabeth reminded herself that there were some great things about being small . . . she was in the front row in every school performance . . . and she could hide in the best places.

"David," Mr. Jenkins said.

"Sorry," David replied in his friendly way.

Elizabeth stroked the soft hamster again, then lifted the edge of her skeleton sweatshirt. She wore a white blouse underneath. "You want to hide?" To her surprise, the hamster disappeared inside. The hamster ran right up her shirt. The tiny feet prickled Elizabeth's skin even through the cloth. Elizabeth grabbed for the moving bump. "She tickles!"

Janna tried to catch the lump, too.

"Gently, girls!" Mr. Jenkins warned. "We don't want a squashed hamster."

The hamster zipped down Elizabeth's arm. Elizabeth sat up on her knees and wiggled.

"Look at Squeaks go!" Anna cried.

Squeaks raced around to Elizabeth's back.

"Help," Elizabeth moaned. "Get her out!" The little claws tickled unbearably. Then Elizabeth felt soft fur against her neck. The hamster must be sticking her nose out of the top of the sweatshirt.

Mr. Jenkins snatched up Squeaks. "Back in your cage, you little pip-squeak!" He set Squeaks down on top of her Lego house, then loosened the collar of his shirt. "Whew, that was some adventure!" The teacher latched the cage door. "So what did you learn about hamster behavior by observing, class?"

"Squeaks likes being inside clothes," someone said.

Elizabeth couldn't seem to make herself listen very well. Small giggly moans kept bubbling out of her mouth.

"She wiggles her whiskers."

"She likes to zip away and explore," Janna added. "She's curious."

Just like me, Elizabeth thought. Her grandfather had often told her that her middle name ought to be curious. Elizabeth Curious McTavish.

The bustling class followed Mr. Jenkins to the library to start their hamster research. Elizabeth's heart finally stopped pounding. She had never been tickled so much in her whole life. At least she was wide awake now. Then she remembered that she should be keeping her eyes open for clues about who had brought Squeaks to their room. The librarian didn't carry a green pen in her pocket, that was for sure.

When Ms. Simm wasn't watching, Elizabeth looked through all the library cards in the checkout basket. None of them had funny M's.

After lunch, Elizabeth's class prepared for the big kickball game. They voted to change their team name to The Squeaks. Since it was warm outdoors, Mr. Jenkins carried the cage out so their new mascot could watch the game, too.

The other team had made a poster covered with pictures of kicking feet. The poster said, "Go, Kickers!" The fourth-graders marched out to the field in step. They chanted, "Kick 'em. Kick 'em." Even Mr. Jenkins's friend Jeffrey looked tough.

"Uh-oh," Janna whispered, then she cheered, "The Squeaks! The Squeaks!" Tom turned three perfect cartwheels, like a cheerleader.

Elizabeth observed every person on the other team to see if any of them knew Squeaks. Jeffrey didn't even glance at the cage, but that could mean anything.

Elizabeth counted her clues on her fingers. She knew about the green ink and the capital M's. Clue number three . . . whoever had brought the hamster probably had the mother hamster, since Squeaks was so young. Four . . . Elizabeth had learned from her research that Squeaks was very calm for a baby, so she must have been handled a lot. The mystery giver loved animals.

Elizabeth played better kickball than she ever had before. So did every one of The Squeaks. "Run faster than the speed of light!" Mr. Jenkins cheered from the sidelines.

They beat the fourth-graders by one point. It was a miracle! After the game, Elizabeth bounded over to the hamster's cage. "You're our good luck charm!" Squeaks cleaned her nose and ears again and again. Her hair stuck straight up on the top of her head.

David sang to the tune of "Row, Row, Row Your Boat," "We have a good luck charm . . . " Janna hurried over to help him make up the rest.

Mr. Jenkins marched back toward the classroom, triumphantly holding the hamster cage out in front of him. Elizabeth skipped forward to be with Squeaks. All the children joined in the song,

"We have a good luck charm.
It's our hamster, Squeaks.
Teacher, teacher, please say yes
So she can be ours for keeps."

Mr. Jenkins rolled his eyes.

As the singing grew louder, Elizabeth saw the hamster scurry underneath her wheel. She lay on her tummy with her legs sticking straight out behind her. Then Squeaks covered both ears with her tiny paws.

4
A Two-Color Family

Hillary stuck to Elizabeth like glue Friday night and all day Saturday. Elizabeth gave her just enough Halloween candy to keep her silent. She didn't want Mom noticing how fast the candy was disappearing. Mom kept smiling and saying things like, "Hillary sure loves her big sister."

Sunday morning, Elizabeth sat in the grass, leaning against their apple tree. Elizabeth liked Sundays because they were family days. Saturdays were errand days.

On the weekends, Mom didn't work at her physical therapy job. All week long she visited people in their homes, helping them recover from accidents. She would finish her visits in time to pick up Hillary from the baby-sitter's and Elizabeth from school, and then do her paper work at home at the kitchen table.

If it was sunny on Sundays, the family did something outdoors. Elizabeth had picked out a bracelet to wear, as usual. Today she'd chosen her duck charm bracelet that Grandpa had given her. Grandpa raised ducks.

Elizabeth balanced her sketch pad on her knees. She kept trying to draw her mom, digging a hole with a shovel. Getting her face right was hard. She could draw the eyes, but not the mouth.

Hillary dropped a bulb in each hole that Mom dug. Bulbs seemed nearly magical to Elizabeth. Why, next spring daffodils would grow in those very places. *Yellow* daffodils. Yellow had always been Elizabeth's favorite color.

Mom and Hillary looked so different side by side. Hillary had brown skin with thick, straight black hair. Mom had white skin with red curly hair that liked to stick out in all directions.

A two-color family . . . that was them.

Elizabeth set aside her drawing. She stood up to help Hillary, who was now dropping bulbs all over the lawn.

Mom turned toward Elizabeth. "What are you thinking about, Beauty?" Beauty was Elizabeth's secret nickname, and Mom hardly called her that anymore, even in private.

"Our family's different." Elizabeth counted on her fingers. "One parent, adopted children, two skin colors."

Mom looked at her in silence for a moment, then squeezed her shoulder with a muddy hand. "A family is people who love each other. You know that."

Elizabeth *did* know. Still, sometimes she had questions inside that she had trouble even putting into words.

Mom kissed Elizabeth's forehead, then handed her the shovel. "Now, daughter, you try to dig a hole."

Elizabeth had to jump on the shovel to make it sink into the earth. Soon she was so dirty that all she thought about was mud and the shovel and pretty flowers next spring.

5
The Squeakmobile

Monday morning, David brought a clear plastic ball to school. Mr. Jenkins twisted the sphere in half and carefully slipped the wiggling hamster inside.

David set the ball on the floor. It had tiny holes all over it. "See, it's a little car for her." Squeaks ran, just as if she were on her wheel. The ball rolled across the floor and bumped into the teacher's desk.

Squeaks spent the hour exploring the room while the class discussed folktales about African animals. Elizabeth kept trying to think of a name for Squeak's new toy. Hamster Car didn't seem clever enough. Neither did the Racer. Then Elizabeth remembered the word *automobile*. Without thinking, she exclaimed, "Let's call it the Squeakmobile!"

The whole class turned and stared at her, even the five children building a game preserve in the corner.

"That's a great idea!" David cried in his usual loud voice.

Mr. Jenkins strolled over to the stuffed rabbit that now sat on the bookcase and had a yellow patch on its ear. "Stuffy," he said. "We seem to have a child who isn't paying attention. Should I put her name on the board?"

"Oh, no," Stuffy answered in a high voice. Actually, it was Mr. Jenkins talking out of the side of his mouth, but everyone pretended it was really the rabbit. "Elizabeth didn't mean to interrupt. Surely, she can concentrate now."

Elizabeth flushed. "Sorry, Mr. Jenkins." After that, she read her folktale about how the elephant got its trunk. She tried to focus on the story, but the hamster kept driving the Squeakmobile around and around her desk. Then Squeaks bumped into her tennis shoe.

Finally, Elizabeth leaned down. Squeaks wiggled her nose and whiskers at her. Elizabeth waved back with her fingers.

"That hamster really likes you," Micah said, his eyes big behind his glasses.

"Squeaks is too old to need a mother," Janna whispered mischievously. Janna was learning about hamster families for her page in their book. "But Elizabeth could be Squeaks's big sister."

"I don't need *another* sister!" Elizabeth replied. Still, it was funny to imagine having a hamster for a sister. Now that would really be an unusual family.

The next day, Elizabeth brought some cheese for Squeaks. The hamster turned the cheese over in her paws and took happy little nibbles. Next, Tom presented a big horseshoe magnet. Squeaks crawled up one side of the magnet and zipped down the other like a slide. She always landed with a poof of dust in the cedar chips.

On Wednesday, they started presenting their pages for the hamster book. Mr. Jenkins spun the class wheel on the wall to see who would go first. Elizabeth bit her lip. The arrow slowed and stopped on *her* name. She shuffled to the front of the room, her head down. "Where do hamsters come from?" she asked. "My page is called The Geography of Hamsters."

"Louder, please," Mr. Jenkins encouraged.

Elizabeth held up the map she'd drawn with her colored pencils. She enjoyed studying about other countries. "Hamsters come from all over Europe and Asia." She pointed at the right places. "Hamsters even live in China."

Elizabeth told about how wild hamsters could be bigger than guinea pigs. "They dig tunnels in farmers' fields and nibble the crops. They are nocturnal animals just like Squeaks. That means they like to be awake at night."

At the end of her report, Mr. Jenkins sauntered up with both hands in his pockets. He pointed to the corner of Elizabeth's drawing. "This little hamster is marvelous. Did you draw it?"

Elizabeth nodded. The little sketch wasn't supposed to be on the map. She had drawn Squeaks when she was bored.

Mr. Jenkins peered more closely. "Perhaps you should consider being an artist, Elizabeth."

"Me?" Elizabeth gasped, but she was pleased. She spun the class wheel quickly. "Your turn, Anna."

Anna talked about how hamsters hoard food. They stuff food into the pouches on the sides of their cheeks and then hide it in a special stash to eat later.

Next, Micah stood up. He wore a white shirt and a tie. He was the only boy who ever dressed up for reports. "My page is on everything that can go wrong with a hamster."

Elizabeth saw Janna's smile, and she grinned, too. That boy would never stop worrying.

"Hamsters can catch colds," Micah began.

Janna made a baby sneeze sound, like a little hamster.

Micah stomped his shiny black oxford. "This is serious! If you have a cold, you should never touch Squeaks. She could get sick."

Elizabeth started listening.

"Hamsters can be eaten by other house pets," Micah continued. "Especially cats."

"Oooohhhh," Tom moaned.

Micah held up a picture of a mother hamster with babies. "This is the worst. Hamsters grow inside their mothers for sixteen days before they are born. Mother hamsters get very nervous. It's important to never touch the babies. The babies will smell like you. Then the mother might get upset and do the wrong thing and eat her own babies."

This time everyone moaned.

"Recess, Munchkins," Mr. Jenkins called out a little early.

Elizabeth raced outside to get in line for the jump rope. She wanted to beat her own record of twenty-seven jumps. Her arms got goose bumps from the cold as she waited her turn. "May I go back inside for my sweater, Mr. Jenkins?"

Mr. Jenkins held his right thumb in the air in his okay signal.

Squeaks was awake, sitting up on top of her magnet, when Elizabeth skipped into the room. That was odd. Squeaks always slept in the afternoon. Elizabeth crossed the room and grabbed her sweater.

She heard *creeaaaakkkk*. Elizabeth spun around toward the classroom door. That's when she saw the new sign on the hamster cage! Suddenly, she heard running foot-steps in the hallway. Elizabeth sprinted for the door, then out to the turn in the hall-way. No one was there. She even stuck her head in the library. Nobody! Whoever it was could run fast!

Elizabeth raced back to the hamster cage to read the note.

This haMster is yours forever.
Take good care of her.

The note was written in orange ink this time.

Elizabeth groaned. She'd been so busy thinking about jumping rope that she hadn't paid attention. The mystery ham-ster giver had probably been hiding in the room when she came inside. Elizabeth picked up the note.

The class trooped into the room, Anna with the soccer ball and David with the jump rope. "What's that?" David yelled.

"There is a new hamster note!" Elizabeth waved the paper in the air.

The children surrounded her to read the words. Micah chewed on the endpieces of his glasses. "*You* could have written this."

"What?" Elizabeth's voice shot up. "I did not!" She turned to look at her friends. Even Tom seemed to be considering the idea.

"Of course she didn't write the note," Janna cried, hands on her hips.

"That could be why Squeaks likes you so much," Anna admitted.

"I heard running footsteps!" Elizabeth argued. "I'm not the one who brought Squeaks."

Half the kids in the class stared at her, doubtfully. They thought she was playing tricks on them!

Then Elizabeth realized something else, and she gasped. "Mr. Jenkins! Now Squeaks *really* doesn't have a home." She felt close to tears. "Oh, Mr. Jenkins, we have to adopt Squeaks."

"Sit down, class," Mr. Jenkins said firmly. When they were all seated, the teacher continued, "I doubt that Elizabeth would have asked permission to come back to the room if she were sneaking in to write a new note."

Micah still looked disbelieving.

Elizabeth hardly heard the rest of the children reading their reports. She kept thinking that Squeaks's owner must not have wanted her. So he had found her a new home. Poor Squeaks. Elizabeth wished she understood why. How could anyone give up such an adorable hamster?

David read his page last. He rolled up his pants so everyone would see his new red socks with hamsters on them. He'd studied hamster food. First, he told how hamsters eat seeds and even peanut butter and honey. Then, David read a story. In his story, a girl named Jenna tasted a hamster's peanut butter treat and shrank to the size of a hamster. Jenna rode the hamster all over the classroom.

Everyone knew that Jenna was really supposed to be Janna. Janna ate a peanut butter sandwich every day for lunch. But they weren't allowed to use names of people in their classroom in their stories.

Everybody clapped at the end. "I'd never eat hamster food," Janna declared with a toss of her head. "Even if it was peanut butter!" Yet she grinned at David.

Janna and David turned to the teacher at the same instant. "Mr. Jenkins, can we keep Squeaks now?"

The teacher hesitated. He straightened the pencils in his pocket. He ran his fingers through his hair. Just then, Squeaks came out of her house. She washed her face sleepily, then scrambled up the magnet and slid down. The teacher laughed. "You are cuter than a crocodile bird!"

Elizabeth half smiled. The crocodile bird

was an animal in Africa that they'd been studying that liked to eat insects off a crocodile's back.

Mr. Jenkins folded his long arms. He seemed to be making up his mind. He gazed seriously at the students, one by one. "You'll have to take good care of Squeaks . . . now that she's your pet."

Everybody laughed and cheered and promised. Elizabeth wished she could turn cartwheels at her desk. She couldn't explain why she loved Squeaks so much. She just did. With all the noise, the hamster raced wildly up the near side of her cage. Elizabeth slipped Squeaks a sunflower seed. She'd take the *best* care of Squeaks.

Elizabeth glanced at Micah out of the corner of her eye. He was watching her. That boy could stay suspicious for ages. Some of the other children might still be wondering, too. Elizabeth couldn't bear them having questions about her.

Now Elizabeth knew that she *had* to be

the one to discover who had brought the hamster. Elizabeth Curious McTavish, *the detective* . . . that's what she would be. More than ever, she needed to solve the Mystery of Squeaks.

6

The Great Escape

Dear Squeaks," Elizabeth wrote in her neatest handwriting that evening. She sat at the kitchen table, doing her homework. Mr. Jenkins had announced that whoever wrote the *best* permission letter could take Squeaks home for the first weekend. They had been studying letter writing.

Hillary sat at the table watching her big sister. Elizabeth rescued her colored pencils from Hillary's fist, then continued . . .

November 3

Dear Squeaks,

My mom and I would like to invite you to our house for the weekend for a GREAT escape from school. We will feed you fancy cheeses and build you a Lego playground.

Our car will pick you up at 3:15 sharp, Friday afternoon. Be awake!

> *With many sunflower seeds,*
> *Elizabeth*

Elizabeth colored a picture of Squeaks and the hamster cage in the bottom corner of her stationery. On the green envelope, she printed *An Invitation to The Great Escape*. Mom signed the letter on the condition that Elizabeth promise to make her bed every day for a *whole month*.

The next morning, Elizabeth slipped the letter into Mr. Jenkins's mailbox. She nervously waited through math and lunch and even afternoon recess. Elizabeth wished she could read Mr. Jenkins's mind as the teacher looked at the letters during silent reading. He kept rolling the end of his tie around his fingers. "I've two stupendous letters," the teacher *finally* declared.

Elizabeth crossed her own fingers and hoped.

"Both letters are well written," the teacher continued. "However, Micah, you forgot to get an adult to sign yours."

Micah groaned and put his head down on his desk.

"So this weekend's honorary hamster keeper is . . . " Mr. Jenkins pulled a green envelope from behind his back.

Elizabeth squealed so loudly that Squeaks stuck her nose out of the window of her house. "Elizabeth's letter *is* written to you," Mr. Jenkins said to the sleepy hamster. The teacher opened the cage door and motioned to Janna. Janna had been appointed Hamster Monitor this week.

While Mr. Jenkins read the letter right

to Squeaks, Janna put some sunflower seeds on top of the Lego house for the hamster's end-of-the-day treat. Only, she didn't give Squeaks just a few seeds, she slipped her a whole handful. "Janna!" Mr. Jenkins exclaimed.

The hamster madly stuffed the seeds into her pouches in the sides of her cheeks. Her cheeks grew fatter and fatter. Finally, Squeaks scurried down to hoard the seeds in her house beneath her favorite rabbit-stuffing bed.

All the next day, Elizabeth watched the clock in her classroom. Mom had promised to get off work early and come get Squeaks. At three, a deep voice said, "Excuse me, I'm here to pick up Squeaks for her Great Escape." The slender figure in the doorway wore a chauffeur's cap and a black suit with a bow tie. Then the person winked at Elizabeth just like . . .

"Mom," Elizabeth breathed. "You fooled me!"

Hillary leaped out from behind Mother. She bounced into the room and threw herself into her big sister's arms.

Elizabeth whispered, "Let go of me!" Then Elizabeth proudly picked up the hamster cage. Hillary walked right behind her, holding onto her jeans pocket with two fingers.

Mr. Jenkins let them leave a few minutes early. *"Hasta la vista,"* he said. "In Spanish that means "See you later . . . alligator!"

"Ciao," said David. "That's good-bye in Italian."

"So long!" Janna cried. Elizabeth knew she *really* wanted to come, too.

"Bye-bye," Hillary answered.

"Adieu," Tom called. "That's French for good-bye."

Mom held open the doors and bowed as Elizabeth walked through. Elizabeth marched up to their car. A sign had been taped to the side window that said *Hamster Hot Rod.* Elizabeth giggled. "This is so wonderful, Mom!" She hopped into the

front seat and held Squeaks' cage on her lap.

"Hillary hold hamster!" Hillary piped from the backseat. She couldn't say her L's, so the words came out, "Hiwawy hode hamster!" Elizabeth just ignored her.

When the car started, Squeaks climbed right up to the top of the cage and started chewing on the wire. "Stop that, you silly hamster," Elizabeth ordered. Squeaks kept right on chewing. Elizabeth had never seen her bite so hard.

The hamster ran on her wheel, zipped into her house to clean her ears with her paws, then climbed up to chew on the cage door. "Mom, she's nervous," Elizabeth said. The hamster ran around the cage and chewed all the way home.

Elizabeth hurried inside her house to put Squeaks on top of the little bookshelf in her room. Perhaps being in a peaceful place would calm her down.

Hillary had followed her. Immediately, she yanked on the latch of the cage door.

"NO, Hillary!" Elizabeth cried, pushing her away. "*Never* open that door."

Her sister's lower lip puckered. Tears formed in her big brown eyes. Elizabeth hated Hillary's heartbroken look. She never knew whether to scream at her sister or pat her shoulder.

Mom decided this would be a good time to take Hillary for a walk. Elizabeth sat by the cage, watching Squeaks chew and chew. Then she thought about how reading always made her feel better. Maybe a book would help Squeaks right now.

So she read a story from *Mrs. Piggle-Wiggle* to her house guest.

"Squeaks is a literary hamster?" Mom asked when she returned. "She likes books?"

"Maybe she'll be an author when she grows up," Elizabeth suggested. She tried to imagine Squeaks holding a miniature pencil or typing on an itsy-bitsy computer.

"Let's see," Mom said. "She could write *The Life and Times of a Hamster*."

"How about *Squeaks Goes to the Circus*?" Elizabeth asked.

"Harry, the Handsome Hamster Hero," Mom mused. "Or how about *Hobo Hamsters*?"

Elizabeth giggled. "Maybe she could write hamster jokes."

By dinnertime, Squeaks had stopped gnawing so hard on the wire. Elizabeth spent the meal trying to think up a real hamster joke. Hillary fell asleep with her elbow in her spaghetti. Mom cleaned her up and slipped her into bed.

After dinner, Elizabeth and Mom tiptoed into the bedroom to sneak the hamster out of the cage. Squeaks was awake, sitting in her food dish. She yawned and showed her curved top tooth. Mom made a cave with her hands against her stomach and carried Squeaks to the living room. "She feels like velvet."

Elizabeth showed Mom how to make a hamster pen on the floor with their legs. She had finally thought of a joke. "What did the goldfish say to the teddy bear hamster?" she asked. Squeaks scurried around the pen.

"I don't know," Mom answered as the hamster climbed onto her lap. "What?"

"Take off your fur coat and come swim with me!"

Mom laughed. "That's a great joke, Beauty."

"Squeaks made it up," Elizabeth pretended. The fluffy hamster waddled down Mom's leg and climbed up over her toes onto Elizabeth's pants. Then Squeaks zipped up her shoulders and sat there just like Elizabeth had imagined on Halloween.

An hour later, Elizabeth drifted to sleep listening to the *squeak-squeak, squeak-squeak* of the hamster wheel. Elizabeth felt pleased, as if tomorrow were her birthday. This whole weekend she could pretend that Squeaks was her very own pet.

7

"No Touch Hamster"

Elizabeth awakened to early morning sunlight streaming into her bedroom. Hillary was already out of bed. She must have climbed in with Mom. Elizabeth stretched, then rolled out of bed to greet Squeaks.

The door on the hamster cage hung straight down . . . *open*. Elizabeth fell to her knees in front of the cage. She didn't believe her eyes. "Squeaks?" The hamster wasn't asleep in her house. She wasn't in her cage. She wasn't even on the floor!

"Hillary!" Elizabeth wailed at the top of

her lungs. "Did you open the hamster cage?" Then she started to cry. Mom came in and sat down beside her. For a long time, Elizabeth couldn't seem to breathe right. Mom rubbed her back. Then she suggested they search the bedrooms.

Hillary walked behind them, repeating, "No touch hamster."

"She usually tells the truth," Mom said.

But Elizabeth didn't believe her sister. Right now she thought of Hillary as a little monster in HER room.

They didn't find the hamster in the bedrooms. They searched behind the couch in the living room, even inside the cupboards in the kitchen. Elizabeth's stomach began to feel sick. What would Mr. Jenkins say when she arrived back at school Monday without Squeaks? She was the honorary hamster keeper! Elizabeth shut herself in her bedroom, alone.

Today was the gathering for the eight families in the city who had adopted Honduran children. They ate a potluck lunch together once a month at each other's houses. Elizabeth usually loved the get-togethers, with all the children.

Today, she begged not to go.

"You can't stay home alone," Mom insisted. "Take your drawing pad if you don't want to talk."

When Elizabeth arrived at the house, she ignored the little children running around with Hillary and sat on the bean bag chair in a corner. She didn't say hello to anyone. She started to sketch a plant, but found herself drawing Squeaks. She drew the hamster sitting up on her back feet eating a carrot.

Nora plopped down beside her, jarring her arm. She was the oldest of the children in the group, already in high school. This was her house. She hung out mostly with the grown-ups so Elizabeth hadn't ever talked much to her. Elizabeth knew that Nora played the flute.

"Is that a teddy bear hamster you're drawing?" Nora asked. "I have one."

"You do?" Elizabeth said. Then she blurted out her own horrible story.

Nora chuckled. "You invited Squeaks on a Great Escape, and she really did escape?"

"It's not funny!" Elizabeth leaped to her feet so fast that her pad of paper went skidding across the floor.

The older girl patted her shoulder. "Want to see my hamster?" Elizabeth followed Nora upstairs, kicking at each step.

"My hamster's name is Amore," Nora introduced. "That means love in Italian."

Elizabeth looked up from her feet. The hamster lay curled in a ball in a high tunnel of her cage. Elizabeth's heart squeezed in her chest. Amore had more white in her fur, and she was bigger . . . but she looked a lot like Squeaks.

"I've been thinking, kiddo," Nora said. "What if I give you some advice about how to catch that hamster?"

8
Flashlight in the Night

When Elizabeth got home, she put twelve sunflower seeds in every little bowl she could find . . . just like Nora had suggested. Then Elizabeth put a bowl in the middle of each room and closed the doors. She stuffed a towel along the bottom of the bathroom door, because she thought Squeaks might be able to squeeze through the gap.

Of course, Hillary opened all the doors right up again. Elizabeth had no choice. She had to keep Hillary occupied. She played Stuffed Animals Having a Party with her sister until bedtime, though she felt more like sending Hillary to Mars.

"I'm glad to see you've forgiven your sister," Mom said.

Before she went to bed, Elizabeth checked the bowls. No seeds were gone. Not one. Then Elizabeth remembered that Squeaks was a nocturnal animal. Maybe she hadn't awakened yet. Elizabeth tried to read her new *Mrs. Piggle-Wiggle* book, but that reminded her of Squeaks, the literary hamster. It took her a long, long time to fall asleep.

Sunday morning, Elizabeth awakened to find her bedroom door open. She could hear Hillary singing in the family room. Still half asleep, Elizabeth counted the sunflower seeds in her room. There were still twelve in the bowl. So Squeaks probably hadn't spent the night in this bedroom.

Next, she checked the kitchen . . . twelve sunflower seeds. She checked the family room. She counted ten sunflower seeds, but she found two more in Hillary's hand.

Every single room still had twelve seeds. Elizabeth swallowed. That meant the plan might not be working.

She waited outside her mother's door until she heard Mom roll over in bed. Then she knocked and zipped inside. "May I count your sunflower seeds, Mom?"

Mom grunted. Only her nose stuck out of the covers.

The bowl didn't seem to be quite in the middle of the room anymore. Then Elizabeth saw the shell of just one sunflower seed in the bowl. "Hurray!!"

"Elizabeth," Mom objected groggily.

Elizabeth reached into the hall to pull another towel out of the closet. She slammed Mom's door and bunched up the towel at the bottom. "You've got the hamster, Mom!"

Mom sat up. "Squeaks is running around in my room, leaving little droppings?! Don't just stand there, find her!"

Elizabeth searched in all her mom's drawers and under the furniture. She didn't find a single trace of the hamster. No chewed-up paper. No little nest. Not even any droppings. "We'll have to wait until tonight." Then Elizabeth explained the rest of the hamster-catching plan to her mother.

Mom even helped keep Hillary out of the bedroom all day.

Elizabeth had to beg, but Mom finally agreed to let her sit up in her bedroom that evening, even though it was a school night. Mom slept on the couch.

Elizabeth filled the pocket of her pajamas with sunflower seeds. She put some more seeds in the bowl. Then Elizabeth sat on the floor of her mother's room with her back against the wall and waited with her flashlight.

It was awfully dark.

She awakened in the middle of the night. For a moment, Elizabeth felt a big lump in her throat, and she had goose bumps all over her arms. Then she remembered. She was sitting in Mom's room trying to catch Squeaks. She must have fallen asleep.

A sound caught her attention. *Scritch-scritch-scritch*. That little noise must have awakened her. Elizabeth knew she should stay still . . . wait to see if an animal ran to the bowl in the middle of the room. But she couldn't wait. What if the noise was Squeaks?

She carefully crawled toward the sound. *Scritch-scritch*. The noise seemed to be coming from the closet. Elizabeth flipped on the light and saw two red EYES staring back at her from the side of a new boot box.

She swallowed a yelp. She certainly hoped this wasn't a mouse. Elizabeth put some sunflower seeds in the palm of her hand and called gently. "Here, Squeaks." She held out her hand and tried to keep it steady. She even shone the flashlight the other way so the brightness wouldn't scare the animal.

A dark shape squeezed out of a chewed hole in the side of the box. Elizabeth couldn't see what it was. She held her breath.

The form came right up to her and put its claws on her hand. Elizabeth felt like her heart stopped beating. The little paws tickled. She carefully inched the light closer until she could see.

Squeaks sat in the middle of her hand, stuffing sunflower seeds into the pouches in the back of her cheeks.

"You crazy hamster," Elizabeth whispered. "You chewed a hole in the box and made a nest in Mom's new boots?!"

9
Promises

"My current event report is about two hundred hamsters and gerbils that got loose at our airport this weekend!" Janna announced Monday morning at school, waving her newspaper clipping. "They were being shipped to pet shops. A box broke. The hamsters and gerbils spread out all over the airport. Attendants found them in cupboards eating food. Passengers found them sitting on chairs, even scurrying down the ramps to get on the airplanes!"

"Two hundred?!" Micah whispered, his eyes even bigger than normal.

Mr. Jenkins tossed a piece of chalk in the air and missed catching it. It landed on his desk. "Enormous hopping elephants! Can you imagine that?"

Elizabeth glanced over at Squeaks, safely sleeping in her cage on Mr. Jenkins's desk. She breathed another sigh of relief. She had decided that she wouldn't tell the class about Squeaks's real escape this weekend . . . or her nighttime flashlight adventure. She didn't want her friends to think that she had nearly lost the class mascot.

Still, Elizabeth couldn't resist another hamster joke. "Maybe some of those hamsters wanted to fly back to Europe or China to visit their wild relatives."

The class laughed. Elizabeth sat up straighter. She had never been able to tell jokes before, not before Squeaks arrived. That whole marvelous morning, Elizabeth concentrated on her schoolwork. She wrote a thank-you note to Nora in her free time, adding a drawing at the bottom.

The class spent the afternoon preparing for the school carnival on Thursday night. This year, the carnival had a rain forest theme, so they all drew rain forest animals. Elizabeth painted a toucan and a tapang tree with her watercolors.

Her whole family must have felt as relaxed that evening as she did. The next morning, Elizabeth awakened first, and sleepily looked at her clock. The red numbers said 7:45. "We overslept!" she screamed, sitting bolt upright in bed. She and Mom and Hillary got out the door in twenty minutes flat. They ate toast in the car and got crumbs on the seats. Elizabeth slammed the car door and raced into the school.

She heard the bedlam in her classroom halfway down the hall. Kids were yelling. Elizabeth tiptoed into her room. What luck!

Not a single person noticed she was tardy. Then Elizabeth froze, still hanging up her backpack . . .

"Squeaks is gone!" Janna wailed. "But I latched the door yesterday. I know I did!"

"Someone must have crept in and let her out." Anna pointed at the hamster cage. Elizabeth stared. The little door hung down . . . open.

"Oh, no! Not again!" Elizabeth exclaimed. The whole class had fallen silent at that very moment. Twenty-one pairs of eyes turned to stare at her.

"Again?" Micah repeated suspiciously.

Elizabeth considered tiptoeing back into the hall. Instead, she told them all about how Squeaks had escaped at home. "I thought my little sister had opened the door!"

Mr. Jenkins got out his magnifying glass and examined the cage. "Why, there are little tooth marks all over the latch on this door! You don't suppose Squeaks unhooked the latch and let herself out?" Mr. Jenkins's voice rose in amazement. "Unbelievable!" The teacher put down the magnifying glass with a thump.

Suddenly, Elizabeth remembered Tom's page in their hamster book, about how hamsters were great at escaping. Maybe this wasn't so impossible.

The class made signs and put them all over the school among their rain forest animals. The signs said:

David taped *Animal on the Loose* right on the principal's door. Elizabeth drew a portrait of Squeaks on each poster and wrote *Please Return to Mr. Jenkins's Class.* She suggested putting out bowls of sunflower seeds, but Mr. Jenkins thought that might attract other "critters."

Just before recess, Janna slipped her hand into the pocket of her sweatshirt she had left on the coat hook overnight. "Oh, yuck, yuck, YUCK," she moaned and showed the teacher a handful of little droppings. Everyone knew that meant Squeaks had climbed up her sweatshirt and stayed in the pocket for a while.

"Our hamster is an acrobat," Micah said, getting out his ruler and measuring the wall. "Can you imagine climbing up something twenty times your height?"

Mr. Jenkins lifted Squeaks's water bottle from the cage. He wired the bottle on the back leg of Anna's chair, closest to the coat hooks. That way Squeaks would at least have water if she was still nearby.

The whole day passed . . . with no word of their hamster. The classroom got quieter than Elizabeth had ever heard it.

Yet the next morning, everyone talked about the carnival more than their missing pet! Elizabeth couldn't believe it. In both of her special classes, *she* spent the time searching every corner and cupboard for Squeaks. The art teacher, Mr. Allen, gave her four warnings to stay in her seat. Then he wrote a note home to her mother.

After school, Elizabeth bit her lower lip and handed over the note. Mom's eyes narrowed. Then she folded the note and said, "We'll discuss this after Hillary is asleep."

Elizabeth didn't enjoy the burritos for dinner, even if they were her favorite food. By the time Mom sat beside her on the couch and asked what had happened, Elizabeth blurted everything out, "Mom, we agreed to keep Squeaks. The whole class promised to take good care of her. We adopted her. Now we've lost her."

Elizabeth's voice rose to a wail. "And nobody even cares very much."

Mom's face softened. She dropped the note and put her arm around Elizabeth. "When you adopt someone you care very much. Just like us, honey. You're my daughter for your whole life."

Elizabeth leaned her head against Mom's shoulder. She'd been talking about Squeaks, not about herself. Still, it felt good to hear those words. "Tell me again about adopting me."

So they got out her adoption book that had all the pictures of her as a baby. They looked at the pictures of the foster family who had raised her for her first nine months while Mom went to court and signed all the papers.

"Your birth mother couldn't give you a home like she wanted you to have," Mom explained. "She couldn't even feed you enough to keep you healthy."

Elizabeth turned the page of her adoption book to the pictures and postcards of

Honduras that Mom had saved. There was one shot of a tree called an elephant tree with a big lizard sitting on it, another of people on a beach, and a third of a village in the mountains. In the fourth picture Mom was holding her as a baby, her eyes shining with joy.

Mom patted Elizabeth's knee as she closed the book. "Would you like to visit the country where you were born someday?"

Elizabeth stared at her mom. She'd thought about going to Honduras, but she'd never had the courage to ask. She had been afraid just asking might hurt Mom's feelings.

Mom smiled gently. "If you want . . . when you're sixteen, we can go to Honduras together. That's my promise to you."

Elizabeth squeezed Mom's fingers. "Nobody could have a better mom in the whole world than you."

10
The Carnival

The custodian fiddled with the bright red bandanna tied around her neck. She had stepped into the classroom, right before Thursday dismissal. "Mr. Jenkins?" She cleared her throat. "I have a private stash of candy in my office." Her freckled face turned pink. "I'm afraid my candy has been disappearing lately."

Elizabeth jiggled in her seat. The custodian had candy at school?

"You think I have a thief in my class?"

Mr. Jenkins let his fiercest gaze sweep over his students.

"Perhaps a four-footed one," Mrs. Brown said. "The teeth marks on the bag are mighty little." The custodian scooped up a piece of paper from the floor and tossed it into the nearest trash can like a basketball. Then she squeezed Micah's shoulder. She was his aunt. "Feel free to set a trap in my office for your teddy bear friend. Hope you don't catch a mouse!" Then she was gone.

The bell rang to mark the end of the school day.

No one in the class moved. Elizabeth felt proud. *They really did care about Squeaks.*

"All right, children." Mr. Jenkins sighed. "Those of you who wish to build a safe trap, meet me at the janitor's office tonight at the carnival. Eight o'clock sharp!"

Elizabeth skipped home. She felt as if she could finally let herself get excited about the carnival. She even helped Hillary get dressed. "There will be cake . . . and balloons!"

"Baboons," Hillary answered.

At the carnival, Elizabeth carried a fistful of tickets. She began by bouncing on the moon walk, pretending she was on the moon. Then she drew butterflies with Hillary. She threw darts at balloons, swung across the swamp on a giant rope, and reached into a chest full of squishy slimy things to pull out a golden necklace.

Next, she headed for the cakewalk room. There were numbers taped onto the rug in a circle. At the end of the music, if the number you were standing on was called, you won a cake. A first-grader had just won a chocolate cake with red sprinkles. He was so excited that he set the cake down on the floor just outside the circle to play again.

Elizabeth waved to Janna. Her friend's mom was in charge of the cakewalk. Elizabeth quickly found an empty place for herself in the game and one for Hillary, too.

Hillary didn't walk. She hopped along to the happy music. Grown-ups smiled and pointed at her. So Hillary danced and twirled. She danced right into the little boy's cake! The people in the room gasped.

"Icky!" Hillary wailed.

As Hillary pulled her foot out, the first-grader screamed, "My cake!" Some older children started laughing. Even adults chuckled.

Hillary stumbled away, leaving chocolate footprints on the rug. Elizabeth grabbed her sister, so she couldn't make more of a mess. Janna's mother offered both of the little children a new cake if they would stop all the screaming.

The boy stomped out of the room with a clown cake, still sniffling and pouting. "I wanted the cake with the *red* sprinkles."

Elizabeth picked out an angel food cake filled with half-melted mint ice cream. She scooped off a fingerful of the icing. A whole cake, just for them!

Mom didn't seem so pleased. She headed home balancing the cake and a very messy, upset Hillary. Janna's mother agreed to take both of the big girls home later.

Elizabeth bounced on the moon walk again until eight o'clock. Then she pushed through the crowds toward the janitor's office in the gym, whistling. Micah was there already, dressed in a white shirt and a bow tie. Elizabeth couldn't believe he'd dressed up for the carnival.

Mr. Jenkins, David, and Janna arrived all together. The teacher unlocked the door. Elizabeth looked around. The little room was *stuffed* with mops and buckets and furniture.

Mr. Jenkins rummaged in the corner until he found a plastic trash can. "This will be good for our trap. The sides are too steep for a little creature to climb out."

Micah grabbed David's hand and tugged him out of the room. They came back a few minutes later with a heavy basket full of kindergarten blocks. The five of them cleared a circle in the middle of the floor. Then they built hamster-sized steps leading up the side of the trash can. Janna balanced the longest block over the top like a high dive.

Elizabeth hurried to their classroom for the bag of sunflower seeds. She dropped seeds in a line leading to the trash can and then more on the block steps. Carefully, she spread a few seeds along the long block to the very tip. Maybe in the middle of the night Squeaks would follow the path of sunflower seeds. Elizabeth dropped a whole handful into the bottom of the trash can.

"Hamster bait." Mr. Jenkins gleefully added a big handful of the janitor's candy corn. Now all Squeaks had to do was leap in after the goodies. The teacher shooed

them all out of the room. "Go home now and get to bed."

Elizabeth hesitated in the doorway with Mr. Jenkins. "Come back to us, Squeaks," she begged in her mind. "Pretty please with sunflower seeds on top?"

The next morning, news about the trap they had built spread like wildfire through the class. Right after lunch count, the custodian hurried into the room. She didn't have an animal in her hand. She had a bright red hand-painted lunch box. "This belong to anybody?"

The children looked disappointed. Even the teacher sighed. Elizabeth raised her hand. "That's mine." She was glad to see her favorite lunch box again. It had been lost for weeks. Mom would be glad, too. However, what she really wanted was Squeaks. Elizabeth stood up to put the lunch box under her coat hook on the floor.

Mrs. Brown pushed her gently back into her seat. "Wait. I want you all to see what happens when you leave food in your lunch box. Open it."

"Oh, Aunt Grace," Micah muttered.

Carefully, Elizabeth unhooked the latch. She held her breath as she opened the box. She knew it would smell of a three-week-old banana. Yet all she saw was a pile of candy corn and sunflower seeds. Where was the banana peel? Was the custodian playing a trick on her?

A pile of candy rustled . . . shifted a bit. Suddenly, a little golden nose poked out of the candy, then beady black eyes. An entire messy golden head emerged. Squeaks had a sunflower seed balanced on top of her fluffy hair.

"There's a hamster in my lunch box!" Elizabeth yelped.

"Wow, Aunt Grace!" Micah cried.

The janitor grinned. "That hamster was sitting on my desk eating a candy corn when I came in this morning. I'm not sure any cage is going to hold her. She must have gotten into your trap *and* back out again."

Several children got up out of their seats and came to surround Elizabeth's desk. Squeaks picked up a candy corn with her tiny perfect paws and started munching from the littlest end.

Just like me, Elizabeth thought. That's the way she liked to eat candy corn. Why, maybe she could take the hamster to the cafeteria in her lunch box everyday. Then Squeaks could eat lunch with the students.

"Mighty fat hamster," the janitor murmured.

Elizabeth stroked Squeaks's soft back. She did seem rounder.

"Well, our escape artist has been eating a lot of candy in the last two days!" Mr. Jenkins exclaimed. He reached into his backpack that was hanging on the back of his chair. The teacher pulled out the biggest chocolate bar Elizabeth had ever seen and sented it with a flourish to Mrs. Brown. "Your reward, madam."

The custodian blushed as bright red as the bandanna tied around her neck. Even her freckles turned red.

11
Squeaks's Greatest Trick

Elizabeth and Janna put on sheets and pretended to be flying hamster ghosts in Elizabeth's dark living room that evening. Janna was spending the night. "I wonder how Squeaks is doing at school?" Janna asked. Mr. Jenkins had given the hamster lots of food for Friday afternoon. Then he had leaned a heavy book against the cage door for extra safety.

Elizabeth stopped "flying."

"I have the oddest feeling that she's up to something," Elizabeth said. "My neck prickles whenever I think about her." They both laughed.

On Monday morning, when Elizabeth got to school, Micah seemed to be herding the other children away from the hamster cage with his arms. Elizabeth pushed past him to greet Squeaks. That boy acted as if he owned their hamster.

Micah poked her with his elbow. "Go ahead, pretend you're innocent. I bet you knew this was going to happen."

"What was going to happen?" Elizabeth answered in a don't-be-silly voice. She looked at the cage. Lying half under Squeaks in the corner were little pink, hairless blobs about as big as the tip of her thumb. "What in the world are those?"

Even the teacher didn't answer. Mr. Jenkins's eyes had narrowed, his irritated look. He chewed on his pencil eraser as he gazed at the calendar. "We've had this hamster for eighteen days."

"Sixteen days is the gestation period, sir," Micah replied.

Elizabeth counted five little hairless blobs. One moved. She gasped. Were they babies?!!!

"You were right," Janna said in her ear. "Squeaks was up to something. Maybe you are psychic!"

Another of the baby blobs wiggled two tiny black legs. Elizabeth stared proudly at the sleeping mother. "Squeaks, this is absolutely your greatest trick ever!"

"Whoever gave us this hamster certainly timed it perfectly." Mr. Jenkins ran his fingers through his hair. "How I wish we knew who our mystery giver was." He rumpled his hair again.

Elizabeth realized with a start that she'd been so involved in searching for Squeaks lately that she'd forgotten to try to solve the mystery of who had brought Squeaks in the first place. She lightly pounded one of her fists into her other hand. From now on, she would look everywhere for clues, not just at school.

Anna bumped into the cage. Squeaks

woke and stared rather wildly at the children.

"Oh, please stop pushing!" Micah half whispered and half wailed. "If Squeaks gets too upset, she might eat her babies."

Mr. Jenkins's face turned positively green. He shooed everyone away from the cage. "We'll leave Squeaks entirely alone."

Elizabeth didn't mind. She could see a lot from her desk. More babies moved. They even started nursing. Elizabeth wished she could see if their eyes were closed, like new kittens.

David raised his hand. "Mr. Jenkins, what are we going to do with these babies?" He hadn't spoken so softly all year.

The teacher stared at the cage for a long moment. "You could hear a pin drop in here," he muttered. "I rather like that. We could take daily notes on the babies' growth and development." Mr. Jenkins stuck both of his hands in his pockets and half smiled. "Why, I suppose we are going to raise the babies, as long as you children can stay as quiet as mice."

Elizabeth started the finger clapping. Then they all cheered . . . very softly . . . so they wouldn't disturb the five new members of their class.

12
The Unexpected Discovery

Those were the quietest days in the history of Mr. Jenkins's third-grade class. Janna and Elizabeth even made a sign for the door:

Shhh!
Babies Growing.
Anyone who enters must tiptoe.

On Tuesday, Squeaks picked her babies up one by one in her mouth and carefully carried them into her Lego house to share her rabbit-stuffing bed. Then, as far as the children could tell, she and the babies just slept. Her food and water disappeared, so Squeaks must have been eating at night. Mr. Jenkins made sure to give her extra food for the four-day weekend.

Elizabeth woke up bright and early on Thanksgiving morning. She dressed in her stretch pants and unicorn sweater and was ready to go to the Honduran Family potluck dinner two hours early. Elizabeth knew it was really too soon for the families to meet again. But they always celebrated Thanksgiving together, then didn't meet until January, when everybody's life had settled down after the holidays.

Elizabeth couldn't wait to see Nora. She helped Mom make the mashed potato casserole by grating cheese over the top. Then Mom sliced all the pickles into quarters to make them a good munching size.

Meanwhile, Elizabeth played hide-and-seek with her little sister. Hillary always got to hide. Elizabeth pretended she didn't see her, even now when the bow in her hair was sticking up over the chair. "Where's Hillary?" Elizabeth called in a voice like a circus announcer. When she got close, Hillary leaped to her feet. Then she ran right at Elizabeth, screaming, "AAAHhhh," at the top of her lungs. The game made Mom laugh until she cried.

Finally, all the food got loaded into the car. Elizabeth jiggled her feet happily as they drove. They were meeting at Nora's again. Most families hosted the group twice a year.

"The January meeting is our turn," Mom said.

Elizabeth was out of the car the moment Mom turned off the keys. She leaped half-way up the steps, then remembered to go back and carry the box of pickles and olives. Mom looked funny balancing Hillary on one hip and holding the mashed potatoes in the other arm.

"Hello, Lydia," Elizabeth said to one of the girls her age. "Hey, Tomás!" Some of the kids had Spanish names, because that was the language spoken in Honduras. Mom had chosen Spanish-sounding middle names for them in honor of their birth country. Elizabeth's middle name was María. Hillary's middle name was Juanita.

Elizabeth plunked her box on the only open space she could find on the kitchen counter and raced upstairs. "Nora!" she called as she ran, sure of her welcome. "Guess what?"

Nora stood beside her music stand, holding her flute. "Hi, kiddo."

Elizabeth told the story of her hamster's new adventure, the Candy Escape she called it. Then she told about the babies.

"Babies," Nora exclaimed. "Are you ever lucky!" She glanced over at Amore, her dark eyes forlorn. Then Nora grinned. "I'm glad my sunflower seed plan worked for you." Her face had changed so fast that Elizabeth wondered if she had imagined the sadness.

Elizabeth skipped over to the hamster's cage. "Hi, Amore." She hopped onto Nora's bed. Her gold quilt was covered with a pattern of musical notes.

"I need to play this piece through one more time." Nora lifted her flute to her lips. "Then I'll talk."

Elizabeth nodded happily. She felt honored that Nora would share her music with her. Besides, she'd been too upset to be curious last time she'd been up here.

Nora had a collection of crystals on her windowsill that glistened in the sunlight. The lilting music sounded beautiful. In such a small room, the flute also sounded surprisingly loud. Elizabeth glanced over at the hamster cage.

Amore was lying flat on her belly with her paws over her ears, just like . . .

Elizabeth gripped the quilt. *Just like* Squeaks . . . just like Squeaks had done when the class had sung so loudly after the kickball game!

Elizabeth suddenly felt every beat of her heart. The thought that was beginning to go through her mind was impossible.

True, Nora did love animals.

True, Nora did have a girl teddy bear hamster . . . that could have been a mother.

The older girl's face looked still with concentration as she played. The singing sounds crashed through the room like waves, washing over Elizabeth with beauty, then rolling away. She looked around the rest of Nora's room.

Nora had two posters on her walls, one of a bright painting of water lilies and the other of a conductor. She had a trophy on her desk. Notes had been taped to the mirror behind the trophy. Elizabeth leaned closer. The notes seemed to be written in different colored inks, one in green . . . another in purple . . . even one written in orange ink.

Clue number three.

The music died into silence. Elizabeth

stood up and walked to the mirror. She couldn't believe her eyes.

"Looking at yourself?" Nora teased.

All the M's on the notes were capitalized!

Elizabeth turned to face the older girl. "You're the mystery hamster giver!"

Nora's soft brown skin deepened into a purple color.

"You're the one who brought us Squeaks!" Elizabeth pointed at her, though she knew that was rude.

"You never told me your hamster's name is *Squeaks*." Nora's voice rose, too. She set her flute on the bookcase. "Your teacher is Mr. Jenkins?"

Elizabeth nodded, her hands on her hips.

"I never guessed." Nora dropped down on her bed, as if her legs wouldn't hold her up. "Then that means I helped save one of my own hamsters two weeks ago when I told you about the sunflower seed plan." She patted the place beside her to show Elizabeth where to sit.

Elizabeth stayed right where she was.

"Why?" she asked. That's all she could get out of her mouth, but her eyes begged. Nora would understand her real question.

Nora took a deep breath. "When Amore had babies, Mom said I couldn't keep *any* of them. Not one! She told me to give the youngsters to the pet shop.

"I tried to think of what was best for the babies. I couldn't bear to give them to the pet shop," Nora said with quiet passion. "I had to be absolutely sure they would have good homes. So I saved my allowance and bought extra cages."

Nora folded her arms across her chest, as if to hug herself. "Mr. Jenkins had been my favorite teacher in grade school, so I knew he would give Squeaks a good home. I gave the other babies . . . " Nora shook her head. "Well, that needs to stay a secret."

She looked up at Elizabeth with a clear gaze, waiting. To Elizabeth's surprise, she didn't feel furious. In fact, she understood. It wasn't that Nora hadn't loved or wanted the babies. And it was safer to give Squeaks to Mr. Jenkins than to a pet shop, a lot safer. She might have done exactly the same thing if it had all happened to her.

Suddenly, Nora yelped. "Oh, no! You told me Squeaks had babies?" Her eyes widened in horror. "I must have left the brothers and sisters together too long."

Elizabeth finally sat beside her on the bed. "Squeaks is okay."

"But she's so young!" Nora sounded like she was about to cry.

"She's a good mother," Elizabeth reassured her.

They sat close together like that all the way until dinner. They talked about hamsters. They talked about school. They talked about Honduras. They even talked about being adopted.

Nora slipped her hand over Elizabeth's. Elizabeth shyly squeezed Nora's fingers. It was nice to know that someone felt the way she did.

"The way I see it," Nora said intensely,

"I have parents now who love me more than anything in the world. I have a great home. And I get to play the flute. And the flute . . . well . . . the flute sings to my heart."

13
Show and Tell

Over the Thanksgiving weekend, Squeaks had been up to her old tricks, as Mr. Jenkins liked to say. When the students came back to school, they discovered Squeaks had escaped again. Only this time, she hadn't escaped alone. She had vanished with all five babies. The little hole they found nibbled through the wires of the top corner of the cage hardly seemed big enough for a cricket to squeeze through . . . let alone a hamster carrying a baby.

"Let's nickname her Houdini," Mr. Jenkins suggested.

Elizabeth figured this was another job for Elizabeth Curious McTavish, the detective. That's the way she thought of herself now. She couldn't let her classmates know her new secret, not for a while. She and Nora had created a great plan to let everyone know how she had solved the Mystery of Squeaks.

During silent reading, Mr. Jenkins heard little scratching sounds in his desk. He opened the bottom drawer . . . and saw all six runaways. Squeaks had made a nest in last week's spelling tests! The tests hadn't even been graded yet. Elizabeth grinned. Maybe Mr. Jenkins would give them all perfect scores.

"Squeaks just wants to learn how to spell," Elizabeth said, raising her hand. "She *is* a literary hamster."

Day by day, the babies grew older in their comfy nest of shredded spelling tests. No one disturbed them. A week later, when the

babies started really crawling, Mr. Jenkins put them back in their own cage. The new mother didn't try to move them again.

Squeaks, however, became a true escape artist. She refused to be caged. One day, Elizabeth found her sitting up on Stuffy's shoulder, nibbling a sunflower seed. Another afternoon, Janna found her curled up on her open book . . . as if Squeaks had been reading *The Mouse and the Motorcycle*.

Squeaks learned how to roll her Squeak-mobile into chair legs. If it broke open, she would run happily around the room. She became famous all over Martin Luther King, Jr. Elementary. The principal, Ms. Hope, came to visit and watch the family. Mrs. Brown continued to bring candy corn. The second-graders even wrote magic hamster stories. Soon the five babies learned to nibble on hamster food and drink water out of the bottle.

At night, the hamster monitor put a thick towel across the bottom of the door, so at least Squeaks couldn't get out into the hallway. Everyone agreed that it was a great year to be part of Mr. Jenkins's class.

Elizabeth finally convinced Mr. Jenkins to let her bring in a hamster expert. On the last period of the day on a Friday close to Christmas, Nora waited in the hallway until Elizabeth announced, "I have a special Show and Tell today." That was Nora's cue. The older girl sauntered into the room.

"Nora!" Mr. Jenkins exclaimed. "What in the name of all the animals that live in the African savannah are *you* doing here?" He shook Nora's hand. "I guess the high school does get out earlier. Class, this is one of my favorite ex-students."

"She was born in Honduras," Elizabeth said proudly. "Just like me."

Nora glanced in the cage at the six sleeping hamsters. "Hmmm, those babies are ready to go home." Then she wrote on the board, "I'M a teddy bear haMster expert."

Micah stood up so fast that he knocked his chair over.

Mr. Jenkins pointed, just like a kid.

"You're the mystery hamster giver! Nora, how could you bring me a pet without asking?"

Nora flushed. Yet she told every bit of her story, just the way she had told Elizabeth at Thanksgiving. By the time she was half finished, Mr. Jenkins had stopped tapping the eraser of his pencil on his desk. He even looked a bit misty-eyed when Nora said he had been her favorite teacher.

Next, Elizabeth explained how she'd followed the clues. Right in the middle of the part about the notes on the mirror, Squeaks woke up. She squeezed through the tiny hole in the top corner of her cage.

Nora watched astonished as the hamster ran across the teacher's desk. She looked at Elizabeth, then Mr. Jenkins. Nora pointed at the hamster, crying, "What . . . ?!"

"She's our *wild* pip-squeak," Janna called.

"Squeaks goes wherever she wants," Elizabeth added.

Squeaks stood up on her back feet and waved her front paws at Nora.

Nora scooped Squeaks up and gave her a kiss right on her nose. "You beautiful baby! Why, you remember me."

"Don't kiss the hamster," Mr. Jenkins cried, pretending to be horrified.

The class roared with laughter.

Amidst the noise, Micah tiptoed up to stand by Elizabeth. "I was wrong about you and that hamster," he admitted softly. He had his white shirt buttoned neatly up to his neck.

Elizabeth tilted her head sideways at the blond-haired boy. That had been a brave thing to say. She wasn't sure she could have admitted being wrong so simply if she had been in his shoes. "It's okay," she said.

Then Elizabeth laughed again as the hamster disappeared up Nora's sleeve. Having the older girl here made her feel special. Elizabeth swallowed, then her heart pounded a bit faster. She had solved the mystery. She had kept their secret until today. She even had a new teenage friend — Nora.

Elizabeth glanced at Janna, her longtime friend. She had just given her a marvelous idea for a name for the new detective agency she had decided to form. Elizabeth could even imagine her sign. She would draw a picture of Squeaks in the corner . . .

Pip-squeak Detective Agency
ALL Animal Mysteries Solved

14
Christmas!

On Christmas morning, Elizabeth opened her eyes to look again at the new hamster cage on her bookcase. She already had the present she wanted most of all. She had one of Squeaks's babies as her very own pet. Micah had taken one home, too . . . and Anna, and David, and Tom.

Elizabeth opened the hamster cage and lifted out Squeaks, Jr. The baby hamster still wasn't any bigger than her thumb. Nora had told her it was a girl.

Elizabeth put the tiny hamster in her

robe pocket. She had to be careful not to scare her, or she would bite. Then Elizabeth skipped out to join her family for Christmas morning.

Christmas had always been a magical time to Elizabeth, full of dreams and surprises. This year, Mom gave her a tent that went over her bed and a special little lamp that she could turn on inside the tent at night. Why, Squeaks Jr. would be able to safely run around the tent with her!

Elizabeth nearly tackled her mother with glee. "Mom! Then you understand that a big sister needs privacy?"

"Sure, Beauty," Mom said.

Hillary joined in the hug like she always did. She had on her new "mouse robe" that Elizabeth had given her for Christmas. Elizabeth tweaked the mouse ears on her sister's hood. Maybe sharing her room with her little sister wouldn't be so impossible after all. Hillary had already learned not to touch the hamster cage.

Squeaks Jr. scurried up Elizabeth's robe

to sit on her shoulder. Mom moved back, looking surprised at the sudden appearance of the little hamster. She must not have known that Squeaks Jr. was in Elizabeth's pocket. Hillary laughed.

Elizabeth looked up at Mom with her rumpled red hair and freckles and down at her sister. "What a family I have," she said. "My very own special two-color family."

Then Elizabeth giggled to herself. Actually — if she counted Squeaks Jr. — she had a three-color family now.